Dog and Bear

TRICKS AND TREATS

Laura Vaccaro Seeger

A NEAL PORTER BOOK
ROARING BROOK PRESS
NEW YORK

For BK, with love

Copyright © 2014 by Laura Vaccaro Seeger

A Neal Porter Book

Published by Roaring Brook Press

Roaring Brook Press is a division of Holtzbrinck Publishing Holdings Limited Partnership

175 Fifth Avenue, New York, New York 10010

The artwork for this book was created using acrylic paint and India ink on watercolor paper.

mackids.com

Library of congress cataloging-in-Publication Data

Seeger, Laura Vaccaro.

[Short stories. Selections]

   Dog and Bear : tricks and treats / Laura Vaccaro Seeger. — First
edition.

      pages cm

   "A Neal Porter Book."

   Summary: "Dog and Bear are back in three new stories, all with a
Halloween theme"— Provided by publisher.

   ISBN 978-1-59643-632-9 (hardcover)

   [1. Halloween—Fiction. 2. Friendship—Fiction. 3. Dogs—Fiction. 4.
Teddy bears—Fiction.] I. Title. II. Title: Tricks and treats.

   PZ7.S4514Doe 2014

   [E]—dc23

                                          2013016658

Roaring Brook Press books may be purchased for business or promotional use. For information
on bulk purchases please contact Macmillan Corporate and Premium Sales Department at
(800) 221-7945 x5442 or by email at specialmarkets@macmillan.com.

First edition 2014

Printed in China by South China Printing Co. Ltd., Dongguan City, Guangdong Province

1   3   5   7   9   10   8   6   4   2

"It's almost Halloween. I can't wait to choose our costumes," said Dog.

"I will try this one," said Bear.

"oh, hello."

"oh, my."

"Dog, Dog!
Come quickly!"

"I just saw another bear,
and he looks just like me."

"NO WAY," SAID DOG.

"It's true. He looks EXACTLY like me!
Please, Dog, let me show you."

"okay, Bear. Show me."

"Look, Dog. There he is!"

"Oh, and he's got a friend who looks EXACTLY like me!" said Dog.

DING DONG

"Hooray!
The trick-or-treaters are here.
Don't get up, Bear. I'll get it."

"All right, Dog."

"Treat, of course."

"More trick-or-treaters!"

Ding dong

Ding dong

Ding dong

Ding dong

Ding dong

"Even more trick-or-treaters!"

"Dog, haven't you given away all the candy by now?" asked Bear.

NO TREATS
FOR YOU

Ding dong

"Trick or treat?"

"No treats for you.
You're not wearing costumes."

"Yes, we ARE," said Dog.

"NO, you're NOT," said Ghost.

"YES, WE ARE!" said Dog and Bear.